Script
JOHN TOMLINSON

Art
GARY ERSKINE

Colouring
SOPHIE HEATH

Wyrdfane Sequences Colouring
DONDIE COX and GARRY LEACH

Lettering
ANNIE PARKHOUSE

Cover
SIMON BISLEY

'Pale hands, pink-tipped, like lotus buds that float
On those cool waters where we used to dwell,
I would have rather felt you round my throat
Crushing out life than waving me farewell'

LAURENCE HOPE,
PALE HANDS I LOVED

'...I CAN ONLY SPECULATE.'

GOD, YOU'RE SUCH A *WORRY-WART*, JO. WHAT DO YOU THINK'S GOING TO HAPPEN?

IT WASN'T A BREAKDOWN, LUV. JUST *EXHAUSTION*— Y'KNOW, OVERWORK, ISABEL BUGGERING OFF AND STUFF. ANYWAY I'M *FINE* NOW. THIS IS JUST A *HOLIDAY*.

OKAY, OKAY. A *WORKING* HOLIDAY.

CAN'T WRAP ME IN COTTON WOOL, JO. AND DON'T CALL ME WAL, I BLOODY *HATE* IT. IT'S *KIERON*.

SIX PAINTINGS. BOOK JACKET ILLOS, Y'KNOW? THOSE '*WYRDFANE*' THINGS ARE COMING BACK OUT IN PAPERBACK.

OH GOD. I ALWAYS *SAID* JOURNALISTS WERE ILLITERATE. THE 'WYRDFANE CYCLE'? BY YOLANDA MARCHANT? SHE *LIVES* UP HERE. YEH.

THE PEAK DISTRICT, YEH. ALL HER BOOKS ARE BASED ON REAL LOCATIONS. IF I CAN CHECK 'EM OUT, SOAK UP THE LOCAL COLOUR, SINK A FEW JARS OF REAL ALE...

SHIT.

NAH— JUST LOST A MINT. LOOK, I BETTER GO, JO. CALL YOU WHEN I GET THERE, OKAY?

I WANT TO WASH MY HANDS.

DON'T THINK ABOUT IT. NEARLY THERE NOW.

THAT'S HOW IT ALWAYS STARTS, ISN'T IT. I ALWAYS START WASHING MY *HANDS*.

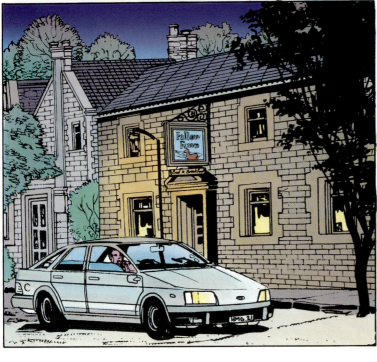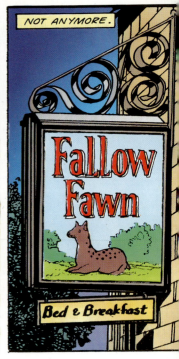

WHEN I WAS STILL QUITE YOUNG, WHEN WE STILL LIVED IN THE HAUNTED HOUSE, MY PARENTS TOOK ME FOR A MEAL WITH AN INDIAN COUPLE THEY KNEW, KRANTI AND MADHU.

NEVER WASH THE BLOOD OFF

ONE OF THE DISHES WAS SOMETHING CALLED 'LADIES' FINGERS.' AS A JOKE, MY FATHER PRETENDED THEY REALLY **WERE** FINGERS.

IT WAS A STUPID MISTAKE. I WAS HORRIFIED, INCONSOLABLE. EVEN WHEN MADHU EXPLAINED PATIENTLY THAT THEY WERE ONLY OKRA — VEGETABLES — I WAS **RIGID** WITH FEAR.

NEVER

MY FATHER, ANGRY AND EMBARRASSED, TRIED TO MAKE ME EAT THEM.

TRIED TO MAKE ME **EAT** THE LADIES' FINGERS.

I HAD HYSTERICS. WE LEFT EARLY, AND AT HOME HE THRASHED ME WITH A BELT FOR SHOWING HIM UP IN FRONT OF HIS FRIENDS.

NEVER WASH IT ALL OFF

THAT NIGHT I LAY AWAKE, AFRAID TO SLEEP.

AND THE NEXT DAY I PISSED IN HIS TEA.

'Dark were the days of the Lords of Misrule, when the High King o' the Peaks held sway over the land of **Wyrdfane** and even **heroes** walked in fear.

'Thence came **Kerowyn** and **Kestrel**, warrior princes born of the icebound North, and their faithful wyvern-pup, **Squablet**.

'Favourites of maids and minstrels alike, these three — for they were heroes all.

'As is the wont of champions, Kerowyn and Kestrel (and Squablet) came to Wyrdfane on a sacred quest...

'...for it was said that the High King held fair princess **Roquindel Goldeneyes** captive in the great tower of **Perivale Castle**.

'Many and strange were the dangers ahead. To reach the castle the princes had first to traverse **The Grips** — ragged jaws of rock that had claimed many a brave soul.

'Legend had it that the arch-fiend **Diabolous** lurked deep in The Grips. Kerowyn and Kestrel (and Squablet), being heroes, were undaunted. Raising their enchanted swords—'

'No sooner had Kerowyn and Kestrel set foot on the treacherous rim of The Grips, than there was a great heaving and trembling in the deeps.'

'Looking up, they saw none other than the old 'un himself — dire Diabolous...'

'Why, said the Prince of Lies, and what have I here? Two fine young callants — and seeking the hand of fair Roquindel Goldeneyes, I'll be bound...'

'I seek hands, too, said the old 'un. And no man shall here pass who has not paid my toll.'

'Why, Kerowyn sternly replied, then we must most gladly oblige! And with that they smote dire Diabolous full-mightily in the eyes!'

'Well, where the old 'un fetched up is anyone's guess...but he had a good long climb back, that much is certain.'

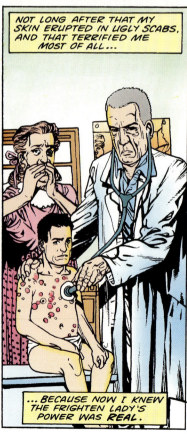

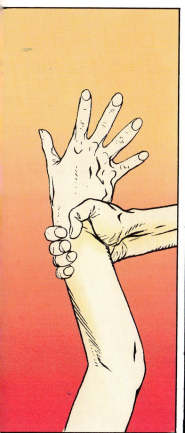

'Long stood brave Kerowyn by the corpses of his fallen kinsmen.

'Till his lips froze to his teeth, his heart a cold stone in his breast, knuckles white with rage on the hilt of Stormsinger.

'For this was none but the dark design of the Sidh.

'The unseen...the old gods... the Lords of Misrule... whatever appellation cloaked their evil, the hand of the Sidh was much in the affairs of men in those elden times.

'They played us like catspaws, nurturing our secret desires, plucking at our deepest, most primal terrors like lute-strings...

'...And they killed us for their sport.

'Kerowyn's unlined brow clouded with the wrath of ages, belying his tender years. On that day his bearing was that of a warrior king.

'Thus did Stormsinger carry the challenge of the three fast friends to the High King o' the Peaks...

'...Thus, that day, did mankind declare War on the Sidh.'

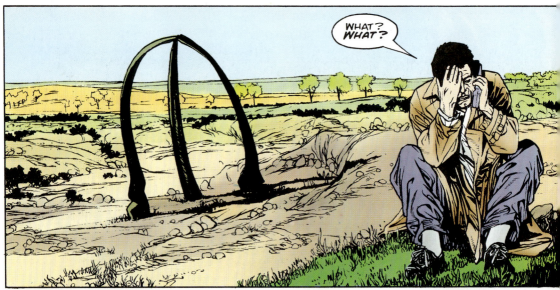

THERE'S A SOUND IN MY HEAD LIKE TEARING; LIKE THE RAGGED BREATHING OF SOMETHING *MONSTROUS*. THE STENCH OF MY OWN FEAR MINGLES WITH THE HEAVY MUSK OF *BLOOD*.

I STUMBLE, UNRESISTING ...AND THEN I'M *BACK* THERE.

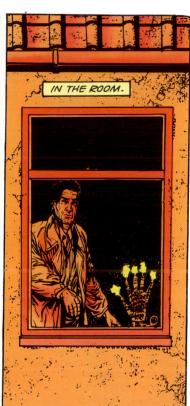

IN THE ROOM.

WITH THE HIGH, WHINNYING CACKLE OF HYENAS, THE WOMEN TEAR AT SOMETHING SLICK AND BRIGHT WITH BLOOD.

THE DEVIL FINDS MISCHIEF FOR IDLE HANDS, SAYS CELANDINE, OVER AND OVER, STRINGS OF RED SALIVA BETWEEN HER FALSE TEETH.

HANDS ON ME. LADIES' FINGERS. THEIR PALSIED, EEL-SLICK **HANDS** ON ME—

COME **SEE**, SAYS THE FRIGHTEN LADY. COME SEE WHAT OLD MOTHER GRUNDY CAN DO WITH KNITTING **NEEDLES**.

REEDY, SNICKERING VOICES DISCUSSING WHAT TO DO... HOW TO **PUNISH** ME. ONE OF THE VOICES IS **NED'S**.

THE TEARING SOUND GROWS LOUDER, AND I HEAR THAT IT **IS** BREATHING, AFTER ALL. THE PREDATOR-REEK OF SLAUGHTERED MEAT IN STEADY WASH AND BACKWASH, PITILESS AS FLAME.

THEN THE HANDS ARE GONE, AND I'M ALONE.

ALONE WITH THE JUDGEMENT OF **BLUEJOHN**.

THE NATURAL ORDER MUST BE PRESERVED. THAT WHICH IS TO BE TAKEN FROM THE FOREST MUST BE PAID FOR, THAT THE TRIBE REMAIN *PURE* IN THE EYES OF THE EARTH GODS.

THE SHAMAN IS SINGING.

A PRIMEVAL OPERA, EVOKING DISTANT DAYS, LOST HEROES, PROUD GENEALOGIES; HIS VERY WORDS AN OFFERING TO THE DEITIES.

RUNES MUST BE CAST.

SACRIFICES MUST BE MADE...

SOMEWHERE AMID ALL THE MESMERIC PRIMORDIAL BEAUTY, I REALISE THAT I'M VERY PROBABLY GOING TO *DIE*.

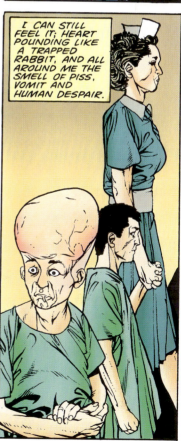

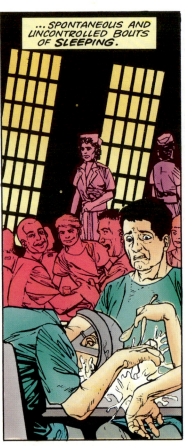

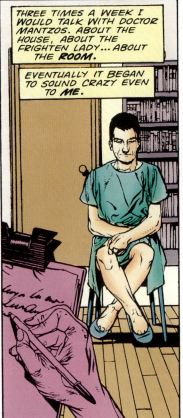

'Cloistered high in dank Perivale Castle was lovely Roquindel Goldeneyes. The knowledge clutched at Kerowyn's brave heart.'

'But the King o' the Peaks had one final obstacle to confound the young heroes.'

'Kerowyn smelled his own burning hair as Balefyr the Twin-Headed unleashed the furnace-heat of his rage...'

'...But Kestrel, faster still, hacked off the Stygian brute's other head. Why, he grinned, how thoughtful of the High King to give us one each!'

'Kerowyn followed suit. Balefyr coughed (twice) and fell, embers already cooling in the great chambers of his breast.'

'Kerowyn knew in an instant that he was gazing into the eyes of his future queen.'

'Fair Roquindel was smitten too, for rare was the maid who could look upon Kerowyn and not love him.'

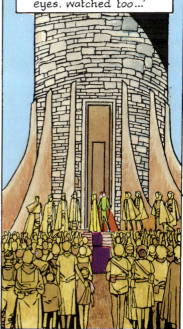
'And all Wyrdfane rejoiced when, a month later, Kerowyn took her as his bride.'

'Above the tableau in Perivale Castle the Lords of Misrule, with baneful eyes, watched too...'

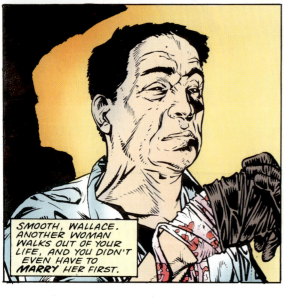

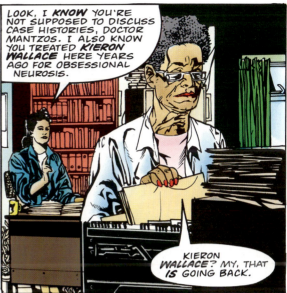

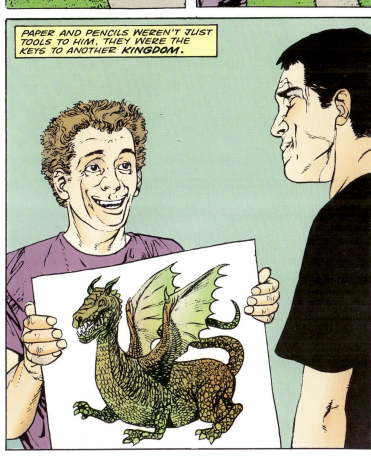

'Savagely he cleaved and scythed at the mocking beast, their bellows of rage, pain and fear borne skyward to the rain-lashed peaks.'

'Yet when he lowered his blade, when at last the brute was still...

...he saw only his own self, with lifeless gaze abstracted, lying cold on the blood-soaked turf.'

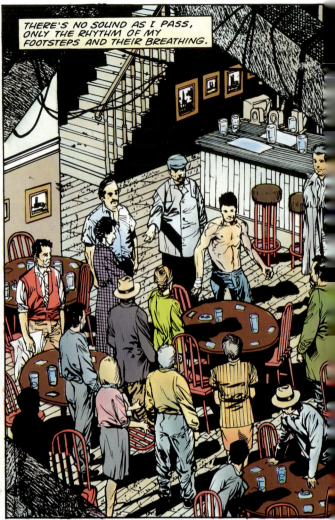

THERE'S A LAYING ON OF HANDS, DEAD THINGS, HANDS OF COLD AND CLAMMY DOUGH, AND I'M OUT OF THE CAR.

SOMEWHERE BEHIND ME I HEAR OLD MOTHER GRUNDY, KNITTING. SOMETHING MISSHAPEN AND OBSCENE, A FUNERAL SHROUD OF RUSTY WIRE AND THINGS ONCE HUMAN.

NO-ONE EVER ESCAPES GUILT.

NOT REALLY. THE VENGEFUL WRAITHS OF PAST SINS RISE UP A THOUSAND TIMES IN A LIFETIME, AND WE PUNISH OURSELVES.

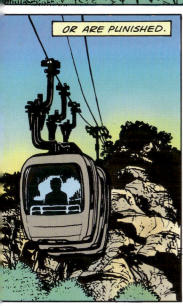

OR ARE PUNISHED.

HE WAS MY FRIEND, I HAD LOVED HIM, AND I HAD DESTROYED HIS LIFE.

ABOVE ME IN THE HEIGHTS OF ABRAHAM WAITS THE JUDGEMENT OF BLUEJOHN.

'I MEAN, I WAS JUST HOOVERING. I NEVER GO IN THERE ANY MORE, NOT SINCE, YOU KNOW—

'NOT SINCE THE BABY DIED.

'GOD ALONE KNOWS HOW HE GOT IN. WE'VE BEEN HERE SIX YEARS NOW, AND — WELL, THEY SAID THIS PLACE HAD A BIT OF A HISTORY, BUT THAT'S JUST A LOT OF RUBBISH, ISN'T IT.

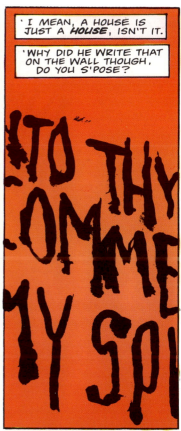
'I MEAN, A HOUSE IS JUST A HOUSE, ISN'T IT.

'WHY DID HE WRITE THAT ON THE WALL THOUGH, DO YOU S'POSE?

'AND JUST LOOK AT HIS FEET. THE POOR LOVE MUST'VE WALKED MILES.

'I'VE—UM—I'VE GOT AN EMBARRASSING CONFESSION TO MAKE TOO, CONSTABLE. I JUST—OH, I JUST FEEL SO SILLY...

'YOU SEE, THE THING IS, I'VE LOOKED ABSOLUTELY EVERYWHERE...'

'Dark were the days of the Lords of Misrule, when the High King o' the Peaks held sway over the land and even **heroes** walked in fear.

'Thus it came to pass that Kerowyn, former warrior king of Wyrdfane, left his sundered realm and journeyed far into the wild, cold lands to the north.

'Long ages past, these icebound wastes had been his home. Perhaps they could be again.

'Perhaps here, in the few years remaining to him, he might come to understand the grim machinations of the Sidh, and find **peace**.

'Little king, said a voice behind him, mocking. Do not imagine you are the first. There were many before you, and there shall be others.

'Many others.

'Why? Kerowyn asked simply. Please, **why**?

'We are the Lords of Misrule, Bluejohn replied. We do as we will, for no better reason than that we **may**.

'Then the wind rose and Kerowyn was alone again among the white-robed mountains, as though none had ever lived there, nor ever could.

HNN.

JOHN TOMLINSON was cloned from a cell-scraping hewn from a Siberian glacier, by a team of pioneering geneticists anxious to discover how the progeny of mankind's Neolithic past would function in post-modern society. Frankly, they were disappointed. To date, Tomlinson's accomplishments consist of a pretty mean chick pea curry and total encyclopaedic recall of all the words to 'The Pointy Birds' by Steve Martin (which, since there are only eleven of them, can hardly be considered a major achievement). Tomlinson's fortunes took an upswing in late 1990 when playboy industrialist Steve White hired him to write an eco-friendly comic strip, *The Knights Of Pendragon*, alongside hell-raising literary firebrand and Martin Amis lookalike, Dan Abnett. Incredible fame followed, and Tomlinson has never looked back since – although it is hoped that radical surgery will soon correct this tragic handicap. He is also the writer of *Armoured Gideon* for Fleetway Editions and co-author of *Digitek* for Marvel, along with numerous other deathless works of modern fiction. *The Lords Of Misrule* represents the culmination of a long-cherished ambition to become the Enid Blyton of horror. Tomlinson is also an accomplished kazoo player, and in his spare time likes to write self-aggrandising by-lines in the third person. He lives in a remote Himalayan mountain cave, on a simple diet of steamed brown rice and yak hearts.

GARY ERSKINE (AKA 'Jocko the Ersk', AKA 'The Rutherglen Acid Bath Murderer') was born on October 23rd 1968 in Glasgow, Scotland. Much of his childhood was spent securely bolted in the attic of the Erskine dynasty's palatial downtown domicile, and is widely thought to have inspired Anneka Lustgarten's 1972 opus, *The Nasty Black Shuttered Dreadful Room*. A two-year course at the Glasgow College of Building and Printing, where he is still fondly remembered in no way at all, was followed by a twelve month stint at the Glasgow branch of Forbidden Planet. Gary remains especially proud of the now-famous 'collapsing shelf' jape, so beloved of visitors young and old, wherein racks of comics and heavy leather-bound graphic novels descend without warning on smiling children, trapping them for several hours. Gary's jaw-droppingly lucrative career began with a strip in Marvel UK's aptly-titled *Strip* magazine, edited by Dan Abnett. This was closely followed by his acclaimed eighteen issue run on *The Knights Of Pendragon*, written by Dan and fellow *Lords Of Misrule* collaborator, John Tomlinson. Other credits include *Warheads*, also for Marvel, and *The Real Robin Hood* for Fleetway. Among his future projects are *Pale Horses* and *Blood Metals* for Atomeka, and a *Punisher/Wolverine* team-up for Marvel US. Gary's many and varied hobbies include wearing dark glasses, slugging tabloid photographers and toe-sucking.

For Janine Johnston.
Ever dance with the Devil in the pale moonlight? John.

For Helen.
Lots of love, Gary.

Under a brooding moon, among the ancient game trails of the primordial woodlands, across the blasted, scoured moors, in the steel and concrete forests, the *Lords of Misrule* will continue their games…Coming in June 1993, a new six-part series by Dan Abnett, John Tomlinson and Peter Snejbjerg. From Atomeka.